CAN YOU SOLVE THE MYSTERY?™

READ THE SOLUTIONS IN YOUR MIRROR

HAWKEYE COLLINS & AMY ADAMS in

THE MYSTERY OF THE HAUNTED HOUSE & OTHER MYSTERIES

by M. MASTERS

Meadowbrook Books
18318 Minnetonka Blvd.
Deephaven, MN 55391

This book is dedicated to all the children across the country who helped us develop the *Can You Solve the Mystery?*™ series.

All characters, events, and locales in these stories are purely fictional. Any resemblances to actual persons, events, or locales are entirely coincidental.

Library of Congress Cataloging in Publication Data

Masters, M.
Hawkeye Collins & Amy Adams in The mystery of the haunted house & other mysteries.

(Can you solve the mystery? ; v. 11)
Contents: The case of the Roman coin — The case of the rich relative — The secret of the mysterious stranger — [etc.]
1. Detective and mystery stories. 2. Children's stories. [1. Mystery and detective stories. 2. Short stories. 3. Literary recreations] I. Title. II. Title: Hawkeye Collins and Amy Adams in The mystery of the haunted house & other mysteries. III. Title: Mystery of the haunted house & other mysteries. IV. Series: Masters, M. Can you solve the mystery? ; no. 11.
PZ7.M42392Hfh 1984 [Fic] 83-27297

ISBN 0-88166-025-6 (pbk.)

10 9 8 7 6 5 4 3 2 1
Printed in the United States of America.

"The Mystery of the Haunted House" by Deborah Felder.
All other stories by Suzanne Lord.
Editorial services by Parachute Press, Inc.
Illustrations by Brett Gadbois.
Cover art by Robert Sauber.

CONTENTS

See details on page 93.

Amy Adams

Hawkeye Collins

Young Sleuths Detect Fun in Mysteries

By Alice Cory
Staff Writer

Lakewood Hills has two new super sleuths watching over its citizens. They are Christopher "Hawkeye" Collins and Amy Amanda Adams, both 12 years old and sixth-grade students at Lakewood Hills Elementary.

Christopher Collins, the popular, blond, blue-eyed sleuth of 128 Crestview Drive, is better known by his nickname, "Hawkeye." His father, Peter Collins, who is an attorney downtown, explains, "We started calling him Hawkeye many years ago because he notices everything, even tiny details. That's what makes him so good at solving mysteries." His mother, Linda Collins, a real estate agent, agrees: "Yes, but he

Sleuths continued on page 4A

Sleuths continued from page 2A

also started to draw at a very early age. His sketches capture everything he sees. He draws clues or the scene of the crime — or anything else that will help solve a mystery."

Amy Adams, a spitfire with red hair and sparkling green eyes, lives right across the street, at 131 Crestview Drive. Known to many as the star of the track team, she is also a star math student. "She's quick of mind, quick of foot and quick of temper," says her teacher, Ted Bronson, chuckling. "And she's never intimidated." Not only do she and Hawkeye share the same birthday, but also the same love of mysteries.

"If something's wrong," says Amy, leaning on her ten-speed, "you just can't look the other way."

"Right," says Hawkeye, pulling his ever-present sketch pad and pencil from his back pocket. "And if we can't solve a case right away, I'll do a drawing of the scene of the crime. When we study my sketch, we can usually figure out what happened."

When the two detectives are not playing video games or soccer (Hawkeye is the captain of the sixth-grade team), they can often be seen biking around town, making sure justice is done. Occasionally aided by Hawkeye's frisky golden retriever, Nosey, and Amy's six-year-old sister, Lucy, they've solved every case they've handled to date.

How did the two get started in the detective business?

It all started last year at Lakewood Hills Elementary's Career Days. There the two met Sergeant Treadwell, one of Lakewood Hills' best-known policemen. Of Hawkeye and Amy, Sergeant Treadwell proudly brags, "They're terrific. Right after we met, one of the teachers had a whole pile of tests stolen. I sure couldn't figure out who had done it, but Hawkeye did one of his sketches and he and Amy had the case solved in five minutes! You can't fool those two."

Sergeant Treadwell adds: "I don't know what Lakewood Hills ever did without Hawkeye and Amy. They've found a dognapped dog, located stolen video games, and cracked many other tough cases. Why, whenever I have a problem I can't solve, I know just where to go — straight to those two super sleuths!"

"They've found a dognapped dog, located stolen video games, and cracked many other tough cases."

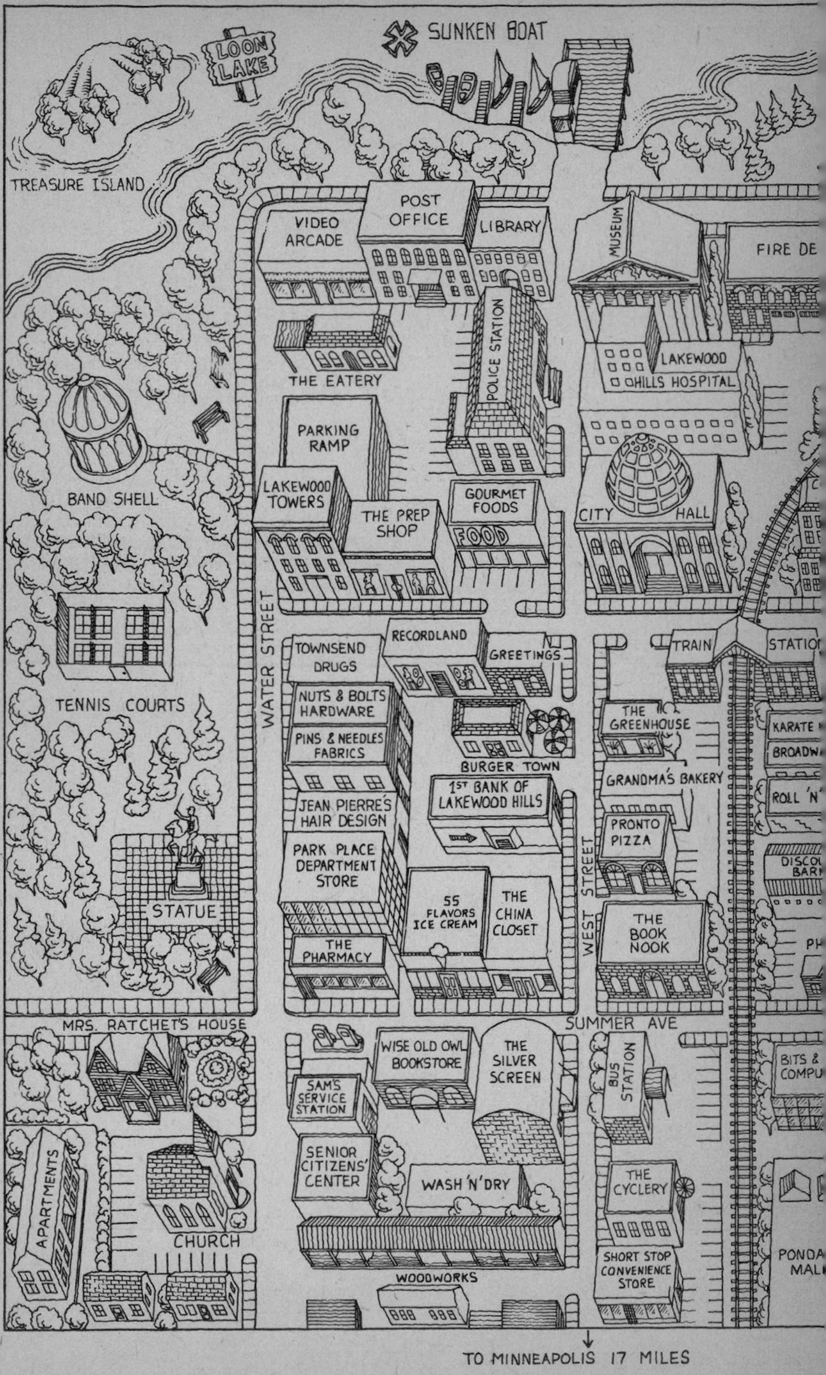

SUNKEN BOAT
LOON LAKE
TREASURE ISLAND
POST OFFICE
VIDEO ARCADE
LIBRARY
MUSEUM
FIRE DE
POLICE STATION
LAKEWOOD HILLS HOSPITAL
THE EATERY
PARKING RAMP
BAND SHELL
LAKEWOOD TOWERS
THE PREP SHOP
GOURMET FOODS
FOOD
CITY HALL
TOWNSEND DRUGS
RECORDLAND
GREETINGS
TRAIN STATION
WATER STREET
NUTS & BOLTS HARDWARE
PINS & NEEDLES FABRICS
BURGER TOWN
THE GREENHOUSE
KARATE
BROADW
TENNIS COURTS
GRANDMA'S BAKERY
ROLL 'N'
1ST BANK OF LAKEWOOD HILLS
JEAN PIERRE'S HAIR DESIGN
PRONTO PIZZA
PARK PLACE DEPARTMENT STORE
DISCOU BARN
WEST STREET
55 FLAVORS ICE CREAM
THE CHINA CLOSET
THE BOOK NOOK
STATUE
THE PHARMACY
PH
MRS. RATCHET'S HOUSE
SUMMER AVE
WISE OLD OWL BOOKSTORE
THE SILVER SCREEN
BUS STATION
BITS & COMPU
SAM'S SERVICE STATION
SENIOR CITIZENS' CENTER
WASH 'N' DRY
THE CYCLERY
APARTMENTS
CHURCH
SHORT STOP CONVENIENCE STORE
PONDA MAL
WOODWORKS
TO MINNEAPOLIS 17 MILES

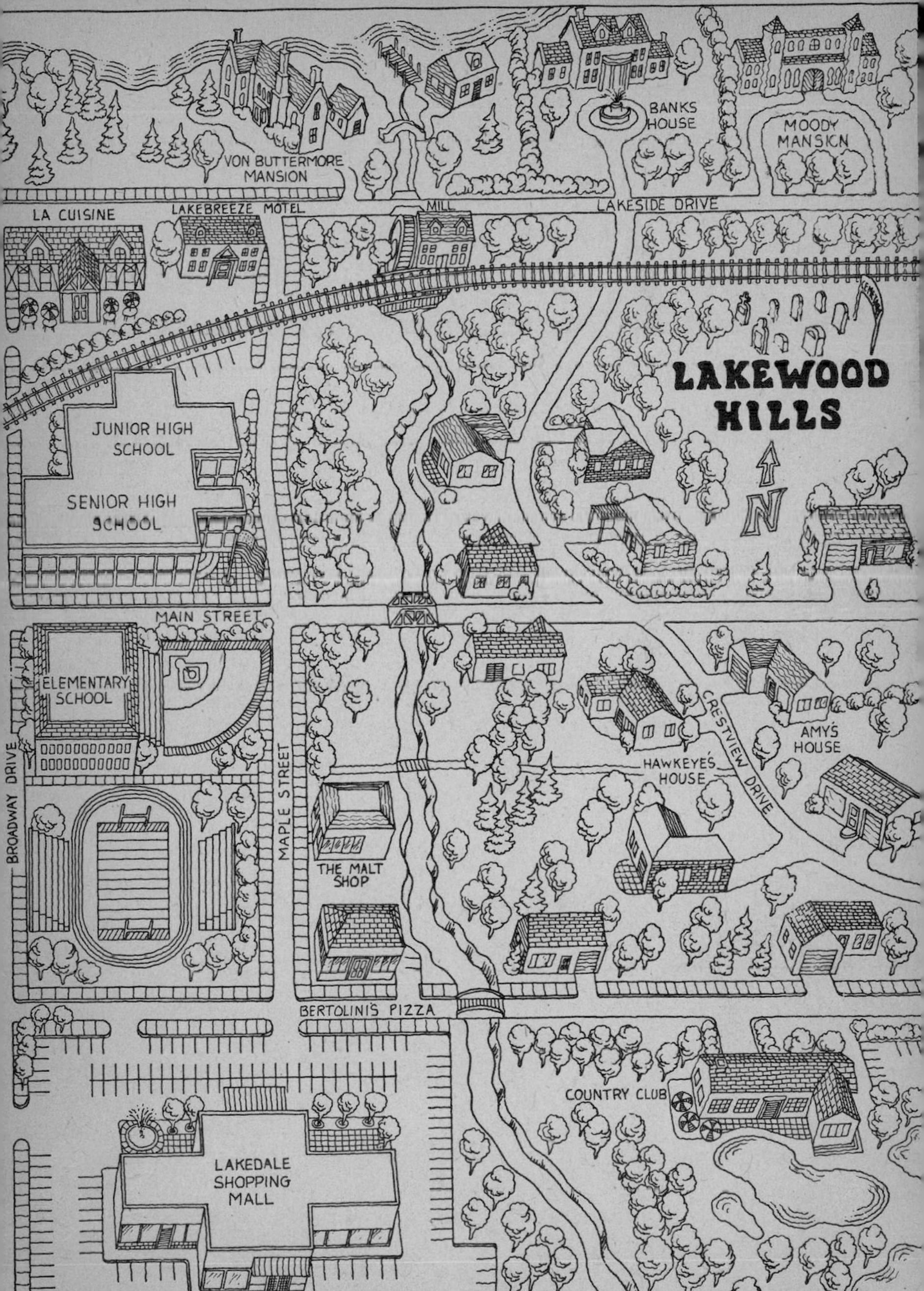

LAKEWOOD HILLS
N
VON BUTTERMORE MANSION
BANKS HOUSE
MOODY MANSION
LA CUISINE
LAKEBREEZE MOTEL
MILL
LAKESIDE DRIVE
JUNIOR HIGH SCHOOL
SENIOR HIGH SCHOOL
MAIN STREET
ELEMENTARY SCHOOL
BROADWAY DRIVE
MAPLE STREET
CRESTVIEW DRIVE
AMY'S HOUSE
HAWKEYE'S HOUSE
THE MALT SHOP
BERTOLINI'S PIZZA
COUNTRY CLUB
LAKEDALE SHOPPING MALL
GADBOIS

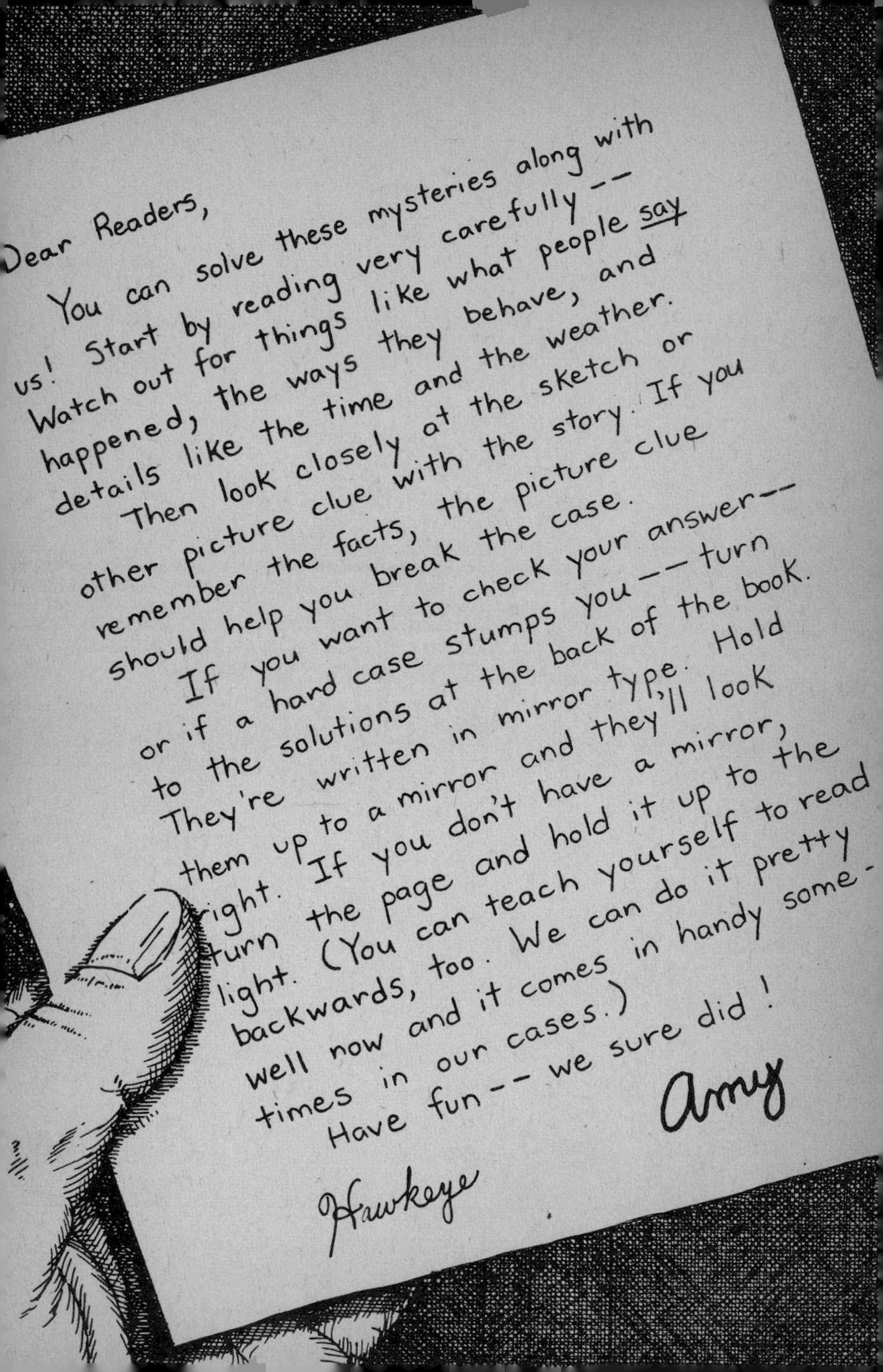

Dear Readers,

You can solve these mysteries along with us! Start by reading very carefully -- Watch out for things like what people <u>say</u> happened, the ways they behave, and details like the time and the weather.

Then look closely at the sketch or other picture clue with the story. If you remember the facts, the picture clue should help you break the case.

If you want to check your answer-- or if a hard case stumps you -- turn to the solutions at the back of the book. They're written in mirror type. Hold them up to a mirror and they'll look right. If you don't have a mirror, turn the page and hold it up to the light. (You can teach yourself to read backwards, too. We can do it pretty well now and it comes in handy sometimes in our cases.)

Have fun -- we sure did!

Amy

Hawkeye

The Case of the Roman Coin

Hawkeye Collins was fooling around with Nosey, his golden retriever, one Saturday morning. He threw a stick across his yard for the dog to chase. Nosey just wagged her tail and looked at Hawkeye.

"What are you looking at me for?" Hawkeye demanded. *"You're* the retriever. Go get the stick!"

Nosey wagged her tail harder and barked excitedly.

Hawkeye laughed, sat down next to the dog, and ruffled her fur. "On a hunting trip, you'd be a duck's best friend."

Just then, he saw Amy Adams, *his* best friend, racing toward him across Crestview Drive.

She looked excited, and Hawkeye wondered what was happening. Together he and Amy were quite a detective team. The two sixth graders had solved many local mysteries, even helping out the Lakewood Hills Police Department at times.

He was sure Amy was onto a big case when she almost rammed into him with her bike and yelled, "Quick, I need a witness."

"A witness?" Hawkeye cried in alarm. "Were you robbed?"

Amy looked at him blankly for a second and then realized that Hawkeye didn't have the faintest idea what she was talking about.

"I'm sorry," she said more calmly. "I guess I was babbling. No, I wasn't robbed."

"Well, whatever's going on has sure got you worked up," Hawkeye said. "Sit down, catch your breath, and explain."

"It's my research paper," Amy said. "I've got a hot lead that might get me an *A*. Each of my last three papers got a *B*. This time I'm writing about old coins, and I intend to get an *A!* I'm doing a special kind of research that you can't do at a library."

"Like robbing an ancient bank?" Hawkeye joked.

"Very funny," Amy said as she got up. "I remembered Mr. Bailey and his coin collection. I called him up, and he said he'd be happy to show me some of his coins. I want you to sketch them, and also be my witness that I didn't just see these ancient coins in a book somewhere."

"OK, OK," Hawkeye said. "I'll get my sketch pad, and we'll go right over to his house."

"Miss Adams?" Mr. Bailey said politely as he answered the door. "I'm so pleased that you want to see my collection. Very few people do."

"This is my friend Hawkeye Collins, Mr. Bailey," Amy explained. "I told you over the phone that he'd be coming along. He's going to sketch some of your coins for me."

"Excellent, excellent! A young writer and a young artist! The coins are this way. Please follow me."

"The young artist is blushing," Amy teased Hawkeye, poking him with her elbow as they followed Mr. Bailey.

"The young writer is going to be front-page news if she doesn't stop bugging me," Hawkeye teased her back.

Mr. Bailey took a glass tray out of a wall safe. He looked at it, then suddenly put it back into the safe.

"I'm very sorry," he said. "I thought this was my tray of Spanish coins, but it's my collection of New York subway tokens! My glasses are being mended, and I'm afraid I can't find my extra pair."

By looking closely at each tray, Mr. Bailey did manage to get the right coins out.

Hawkeye was surprised at how many different

kinds of coins Mr. Bailey had in his collection. He and Amy looked at Indian-head pennies, buffalo nickels, Eisenhower dollars, gold coins from the 1800s, and Colonial coins.

"I'm glad you needed me for a witness," Hawkeye told Amy. "This coin collection is great!"

The telephone rang, and Mr. Bailey went to answer it. When he returned, his eyes were shining. "That was a coin dealer," he told his guests. "I do hope you'll stay to see what he's bringing over. It's an unusual Roman coin. The dealer says it was minted in 100 B.C."

Amy's eyes almost popped out of her head. "That means it's more than two thousand years old!" she cried.

While they were waiting for the coin dealer, Amy and Hawkeye looked at Mr. Bailey's tray of old Greek and Roman coins. "It's weird to think that people really bought things with these," Amy said.

"Yes," Mr. Bailey agreed. "I enjoy imagining who might have held each coin and what might have been bought with it."

When the coin dealer arrived, he got right down to business.

"Let me tell you the history of the coin," he told Mr. Bailey. "According to legend, an ancient Roman got himself into some sort of trouble. He buried the coins, intending to go back and get them later. But he never returned. For centuries, people looked for the coins.

"The current owner of the grounds where the coins were supposed to be buried did some digging on his own," the dealer continued. "After three summers of digging, he found what he was looking for!

"The coins must have been buried right after they were minted. They were never used. They stayed in perfect condition while they were buried. These are the best preserved coins in the world!"

"Wow! What a story," Amy said in awe.

"Do you have one of the coins?" Hawkeye asked.

"Of course," the dealer said, reaching into an inner pocket of his jacket. He brought out a small box, much like a ring box, and opened it. Nestled in the box was a shiny coin.

"Why, it looks like new!" exclaimed Mr. Bailey, squinting at the gold coin.

Hawkeye was sketching as fast as he could. "May we see the other side?"

"Surely," the dealer said, and he turned the coin over. Hawkeye quickly sketched the other side.

"I'd like some time to decide if I want to buy the coin," said Mr. Bailey. "The price you named on the phone is more than I'm used to paying."

"Maybe so," the dealer said cheerfully. "But remember that this coin is in better condition than you're used to seeing!"

"It's an unusual Roman coin," Mr. Bailey said.

As Mr. Bailey showed the dealer to the door, Hawkeye motioned Amy over to his side. "I think Mr. Bailey had better find his glasses fast," he said.

"Is something wrong?" Amy asked.

"You bet! Mr. Bailey is so impressed with this coin that it'll be hard to tell him it's a fake. But the only thing I'm impressed with is that dealer's nerve!"

WHY DID HAWKEYE BELIEVE THE COIN WAS A FAKE?

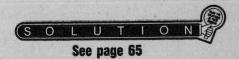

S O L U T I O N

See page 65

The Case of the Rich Relative

"Hi, Sarge," Amy called as she and Hawkeye rode their bikes past the police station.

"Huh? Oh, hi, kids," said Sarge sleepily as he headed toward the front steps of the station.

"Gee, you look exhausted!" said Amy. "Big case?" Sergeant Treadwell liked to tell Hawkeye and Amy about his cases, and they liked hearing about them.

"Big headache," Sarge corrected her. "Ever since that inheritance ad ran in the daily paper, I haven't had a moment's peace!"

"What ad?" Hawkeye asked. "What inheritance?"

Amy turned to him. "Where have you been

all week? Under a rock? It's all everyone's been talking about!

"There was a Mr. Alvarez living here about forty years ago," she explained. "He left Lakewood Hills and made a fortune in South America. He never got married, so he had no wife or kids to leave his money to when he died. He left everything to a nephew who still lives around here somewhere—but nobody is sure where. Mr. Alvarez's lawyer has put ads in the local papers, searching for the missing nephew."

"And you're getting a lot of calls, huh, Sarge?" Hawkeye asked.

"The phones are ringing off the wall! People will do anything to get some easy money. You'd think everyone in town was related to Alvarez."

"How are you ever going to sift through the cranks and find the real relative?" Amy asked.

"Actually," Sarge said, brightening, "that's the easiest part! We have some inside information about the real relative. He has a condition that a crank wouldn't know about."

A policeman called to Sarge from the entrance of the station. "We think we've got a good lead," the man said. "Look at this letter."

Sarge looked at the letter carefully. "This might be it! Want to come along and help me check it out?" he asked Amy and Hawkeye.

"Boy, Sarge, you ought to put us on salary," Amy teased him.

"Wait a few years," Sarge said with a smile. "Leave your bikes in the station house, and we'll ride over in my car."

"Why are you so sure this is the right person?" Hawkeye asked on the way.

"Because of the special condition of Mr. Alvarez's relative. He's deaf! That's why the announcement was in the paper, and why we knew the real nephew wouldn't contact the station house by phone."

When they arrived at the address given in the letter, Sarge knocked on the door.

"Uh, Sarge," Amy said, "he won't hear that."

Sarge reddened in embarrassment.

But to everyone's surprise, the door *was* answered—promptly. "Mr. Alvarez? How did you hear me knocking?" Sarge blurted out.

The man smiled and pointed to a dog beside him.

"A hearing-aid dog," Hawkeye said. "I've read about them. They're like guide dogs for the blind, only they hear things instead. The dog can wake a person up when an alarm clock goes off, let him know if someone's knocking on the door or if water is boiling, or—"

"We get the idea!" Amy said with a laugh.

Sarge got a pad and pencil out of his pocket and wrote down his own name, then Amy's and Hawkeye's.

"You don't have to bother writing everything,"

the man said. "I read lips. If my back is turned, just tap me on the shoulder. OK?"

"Got it," Sarge said.

"And," the man said, "my name is Daniel Mareno, not Alvarez. Mr. Alvarez was an uncle on my mother's side of the family."

Sarge smiled. "Well, you've already answered my first question correctly. I hope you don't mind a lot of questions. We have to make sure we have the right person. There are certain facts to be checked that only Mr. Alvarez's relative would know."

Mr. Mareno showed everyone into the living room. "Please excuse the clutter. I'm an inventor, and I like to keep all kinds of spare parts handy." Then he went into the kitchen to get some refreshments.

"Seems like a nice guy," Sarge said.

"If he's the missing relative," Amy said, "he can *afford* to be nice!"

Mr. Mareno came back with milk and cookies for Amy and Hawkeye and some coffee for himself and Sarge. Then he sat facing Sarge so that he could clearly see the officer's lips.

While Sarge asked his questions, Amy nudged Hawkeye. "I'm going to try something," she murmured. "Watch Mr. Mareno and see if he reacts."

She picked up her glass and plate and took them into the kitchen. When she came back, she was directly behind Mr. Mareno. She took a key chain out of her jeans pocket and dropped it on the floor.

The dog turned around at the sudden noise, and Sarge jumped a mile—but Mr. Mareno only looked puzzled at Sarge's reaction.

"Sorry," Amy said. "Dropped my keys."

She rejoined Hawkeye. "He never flinched," Hawkeye whispered.

"Then why do I have this funny feeling?" Amy asked irritably.

"Because you're a funny person?" Hawkeye joked.

"I'm not kidding, Hawkeye. Something just doesn't feel right about all this. Would you please do some sketches?"

Hawkeye nodded, pulled out his sketch pad, and quickly went to work.

After a few more minutes, Sarge completed his questioning. "That's good enough for me," he said happily. "I can't tell you, Mr. Mareno, how glad I'll be to close this case. I can get some rest from all those phonies calling in!"

Mr. Mareno smiled. "More coffee?" he offered.

"No, thanks," Sarge said. "I've got to get back to the station house. The faster I file this report, the faster I close this case—and the faster you'll collect your inheritance."

Mr. Mareno grinned at that, and showed them to the door.

"Something doesn't feel right about all this," said Amy. "Would you please do some sketches?"

In the car, Sarge mopped his brow. "I don't mind telling you, when Mr. Mareno answered the door like that, my heart sank. I was afraid we were back at square one!"

"Let me see those sketches, Hawkeye," Amy said. Hawkeye had made four sketches of the room.

"I thought so!" Amy exclaimed when she got to the third sketch.

"Oh, no!" Sarge moaned. "Don't tell me you found something wrong!"

"All right, I won't tell you."

Sarge looked as though his whole day had caved in. "Go ahead—tell me," he said dejectedly.

"I'm sorry," Amy said, "but that man *isn't* Mr. Mareno. Still, you're not back at square one. He probably knows Mr. Mareno to know so much about his family—and to know about his deafness."

"Thanks for that small consolation," Sarge said. "But why don't you think that man is Mr. Mareno?"

"Because he's not deaf!"

WHY WAS AMY SO CERTAIN THE MAN WASN'T DEAF?

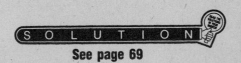

SOLUTION
See page 69

The Secret of the Mysterious Stranger

"Amy," Mrs. Adams called. "Telephone. It's Hawkeye."

"In a minute, Mom."

"Amy Amanda—"

"Coming!" Amy said, jumping up. When her mother used Amy's full name, it was time to move!

Amy hurried to the upstairs extension. "Hi, Hawkeye. What's up?"

"My parents are acting very weird, that's what."

"So what else is new?" Amy said. "Parents are always acting weird."

"Not like this. I'm at the Pondale Mall. Meet me out in front in twenty minutes, and I'll tell you all about it. Don't be late, Amy!"

"Hey, wait a min—" Amy looked at the phone in disbelief. Hawkeye had hung up on her!

When Amy rode her ten-speed up to the mall, Hawkeye was waiting impatiently for her.

"What's the matter, Hawkeye? Is it something serious?"

"I don't think so," Hawkeye said. "It has something to do with Pat McDonald, an old friend of our family's.

"My parents and this Pat McDonald used to run around in the same group of friends, like kids at school do nowadays," Hawkeye explained. "Well, Pat got a really good job in New York and moved there. Now he's a big executive or something, and he's coming to Minneapolis on business. We're going to meet him at the airport. My folks are really excited. It's been years since they've seen this guy."

"What's so weird about meeting an old friend at the airport?" Amy asked.

"What's weird is the way my folks are acting toward *me*. I told them that I remembered Pat, even though I was little the last time I saw him. Now every time I say something about this guy, they start to crack up laughing. Whatever the joke is, I'm not in on it!"

"Maybe you're just saying his name funny," Amy suggested.

"C'mon, Amy, I am not. There's no way to

say the name 'McDonald' funny."

"I see what you mean," Amy agreed. "Are you sure you remember the guy?"

"Positive," Hawkeye said. "Listen, Amy. Whatever's going on, we should be able to figure it out. Come to the airport with me. One of us should be able to spot something to explain my folks' weird behavior."

"No problem," said Amy. "We'll find out what's so funny about Pat McDonald!"

"While we park the car, Hawkeye, you and Amy go ahead and meet the plane," said Mr. Collins. "It'll be a great surprise for Pat, who used to call you Baby Christopher, to be greeted by a grown-up sixth grader."

"But, Dad," Hawkeye said, "I don't know what Mr. McDonald looks like! It's been a long time since I've seen him."

Amy saw Mrs. Collins hide a smirk. Mr. Collins was having a hard time choking back laughter. Hawkeye was right, she realized. Something strange was definitely going on!

"Don't worry," said Mrs. Collins. "We have this letter from Pat that gives a pretty good description."

"I'm still tall and, believe it or not, still thin. But my hair is silver now! I'll wear a dark suit and a hat with a pheasant feather on it, and I'll be carrying my ever-present briefcase. Can't wait to see you all, especially Christopher!"

"Plus," Mr. Collins added, "Pat travels first-class and should be one of the first people off the plane."

"Dad let me bring his instant camera to take pictures of the big reunion," Amy said cheerfully.

"Great!" said Mrs. Collins. "Be sure to get a picture of Pat and Hawkeye meeting." And she put her hand over her mouth to try and hide the big grin on her face.

When Hawkeye's folks headed toward the huge parking ramp, he and Amy hurried through the airport to the right arrival gate.

"Here they come," Amy said excitedly. "I'll take a photograph of the first passengers as they come out. Pat McDonald will surely be one of them."

When the first group of passengers came into view, Amy carefully snapped a picture. "That should do it," she said.

Hawkeye was busy using his sharp eyes to compare all the details he was seeing with the description of Pat McDonald.

"Amy, everybody out there seems to be wearing a dark suit and carrying a briefcase," he muttered. "I've never seen so many hats with little feathers on them—on so many silver-headed people. And nobody looks familiar at all!"

"C'mon, Hawkeye. Reason it out—like you do any mystery. You can find him."

"Wait a sec!" said Hawkeye, grinning. "I'll have him paged!"

"Now you're thinking!" Amy cheered.

As Hawkeye moved toward the crowded information desk, Amy studied her just-developed picture of the arriving passengers. She suddenly burst into laughter and ran after Hawkeye. When she tapped him on the shoulder and he turned around, she tried hard to stop giggling.

"What's so funny?" Hawkeye asked, puzzled.

"Pat McDonald," Amy said, and she started laughing again. "Are you *positive* that you remember him?"

"Amy! Now you're acting just like my folks!" Hawkeye cried. "You're supposed to be helping me. If you're my friend, you'll tell me which guy is Pat McDonald!"

"OK. None of them are."

"You mean he didn't come?" Hawkeye asked.

"No. Pat McDonald is here, all right."

"But you just said—"

At that moment, a clerk at the information desk turned to Hawkeye. "Would you please page Pat McDonald?" Hawkeye requested.

"PAGING PAT MCDONALD," the loudspeaker blared. "WILL PAT MCDONALD PLEASE STEP TO THE INFORMATION DESK."

"Quick, Hawkeye. Look at this picture I took. Take a good, close look." Amy shoved the photo

When the first group of passengers came into view, Amy carefully snapped a picture.

into his hands and waited.

Hawkeye studied the photo, thought for a moment, and then groaned. "Of course! Pat McDonald *is* here—and fits the description exactly!"

WHICH ONE OF THE PASSENGERS WAS PAT MCDONALD?

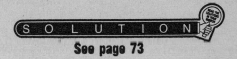

SOLUTION

See page 73

The Secret of the Special Spies

Hawkeye sat down in front of Dr. Adams's home computer terminal and sighed. "I thought doing a report on my own family's history would be easy," he complained. "Boy, was I wrong! My family's so—so dull!"

Amy, waiting for a printout of her own history report, stared at him. "C'mon, Hawkeye. Your family's great."

"Oh, they're nice people," Hawkeye said glumly, "but interesting? No way! Your mother's a doctor, and your dad's a pilot. Now *that's* interesting.

"My dad's a lawyer, and my mom sells real estate. I'm telling you, this report is doomed!"

"Quit it, Hawkeye!" ordered Amy. "Your father has worked on some terrific cases. And your mom's responsible for lots of people moving here instead of somewhere else."

"All right, all right," Hawkeye gave in. "You've convinced me. My family is the best thing that's happened to Lakewood Hills since the creation of the hot fudge sundae!"

"That's a slight exaggeration," Amy said with a grin. "But speaking of food, want something to eat?"

During lunch in the school cafeteria the next day, Hawkeye, Amy, and some of their classmates discussed the history assignment.

"Ready for the big report?" Amy asked Hawkeye.

"As ready as I'll ever be," replied Hawkeye. "It wasn't as tough—"

"I'm ready!" a voice interrupted.

Hawkeye and Amy stared across the table at Mark Evinrude, one of their least favorite classmates. Mark's parents were the biggest snobs in Lakewood Hills. They were extremely proud of their ancestors and felt that their family was better than almost every other one in town.

Mark wasn't quite as bad as his parents, but he was used to bragging a lot about his family's background.

"Which branch of your family are you writing about?" Hawkeye asked in a bored voice. "The ones that set up all thirteen original colonies?"

Mark gave Hawkeye a disgusted look. "Well, I'll bet that none of *your* ancestors were spies during the American Revolution!"

Hawkeye got a sinking feeling in the pit of his stomach. "Great," he mumbled to Amy. "Next to that, my report should have all the flash of an unplugged video game."

"Mark," Amy said, "this is supposed to be a report, remember? It's not just a story-writing contest."

"It's *true*—and I can prove it!"

Eagerly, Mark started explaining. "My ancestors were, of course, in the upper crust of society during Colonial times."

"They were probably some of the biggest crumbs," Hawkeye said under his breath. Amy's green eyes twinkled with laughter, but she kept quiet. Mark rattled on.

"The British thought my family was loyal to England. But George Washington knew that they were really in favor of the Revolution.

"So while they pretended to be on the side of the British, my ancestors were actually spying for the Americans! They passed along important messages—right under the noses of the British. Why, if it hadn't been for my ancestors, half of Washington's troops wouldn't have known where to go, or when to get there!"

"That's fascinating, Mark," Amy said. "Was your family rewarded for what they did?"

"Uh-uh. To everyone who knew them, my ancestors had appeared to side with the British. When the war ended, they received threats from people who didn't believe that they had really been working for the Revolution."

"You said you could prove your story," Amy said. "How?"

"I've got a letter of thanks that was sent to my ancestors—and it was written by George Washington himself!"

Hawkeye rolled his eyes in disbelief. "Oh, come *on,* Mark! Enough is enough!"

Mark ignored him. "My parents gave me special permission to bring it to school just this once. I'll show it to you if you promise not to touch it."

Hawkeye and Amy agreed. Mark opened his backpack on the bench beside him and took out an object wrapped in cloth. Under the cloth and framed behind glass was a letter to Hezekiah Evinrude. The paper, the ink, and the writing all looked very old.

"Wow!" Amy said, pointing to the signature. "It *is* signed by George Washington!"

Hawkeye was busy reading the letter. When he finished, he was strangely quiet.

"Well," Mark asked proudly, "what do you think of that? Obviously, George Washington had great respect for my family."

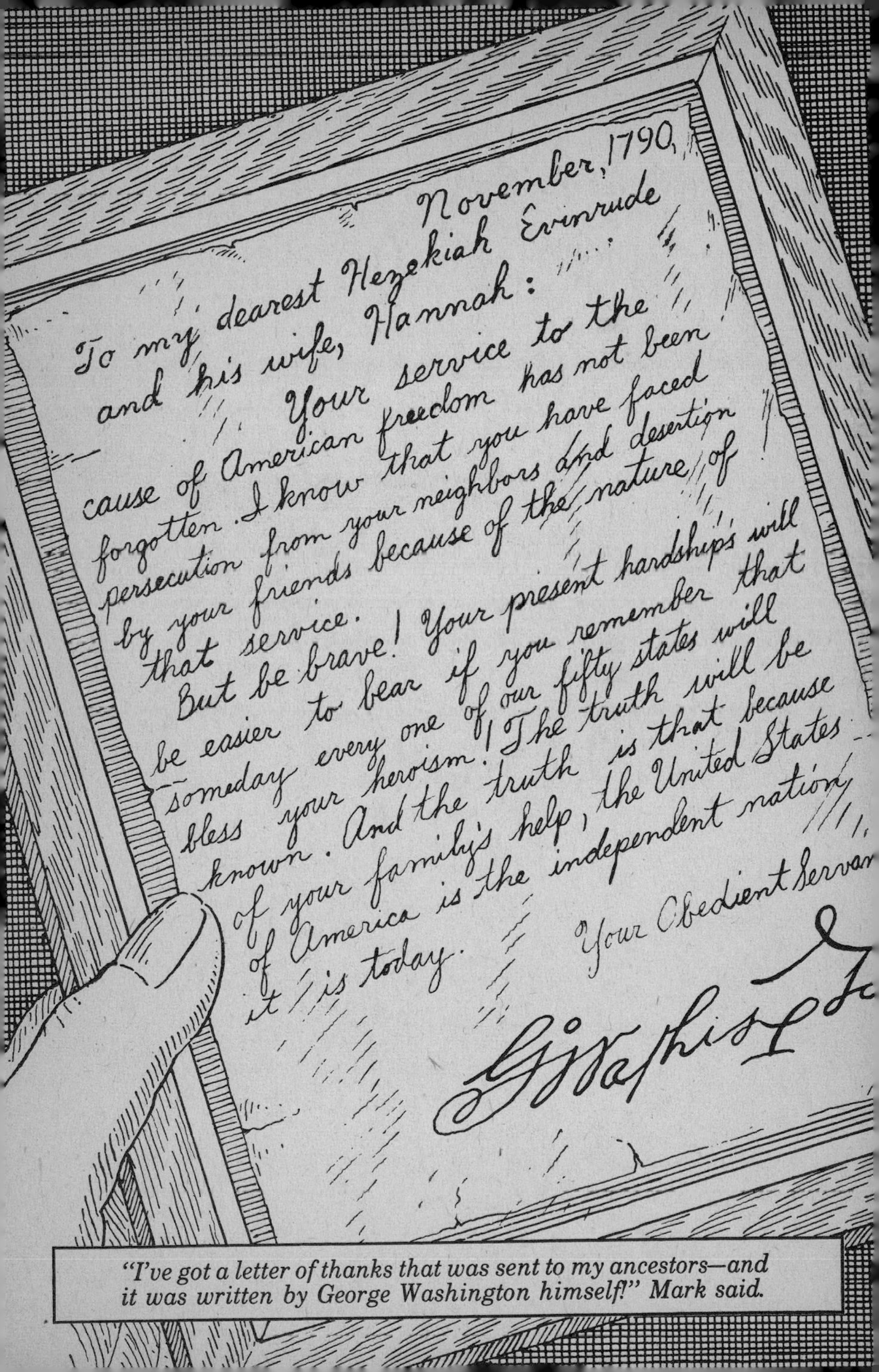
November, 1790,
To my dearest Hezekiah Evinrude
and his wife, Hannah:
Your service to the
cause of American freedom has not been
forgotten. I know that you have faced
persecution from your neighbors and desertion
by your friends because of the nature of
that service.
But be brave! Your present hardships will
be easier to bear if you remember that
someday every one of our fifty states will
bless your heroism! The truth will be
known. And the truth is that because
of your family's help, the United States
of America is the independent nation
it is today.
Your Obedient Servan

"I've got a letter of thanks that was sent to my ancestors—and it was written by George Washington himself!" Mark said.

Hawkeye looked Mark straight in the eye. “The only thing obvious about this letter,” he said, “is that it couldn’t have been written by George Washington!”

WHY DID HAWKEYE THINK THE LETTER WAS A FAKE?

SOLUTION
See page 77

The Mystery of the Haunted House

Something was wrong, and Hawkeye couldn't figure out what it was. All through dinner, his mom had been very quiet, and she hadn't eaten much. At the moment, she was staring at her plate.

Mr. Collins had noticed it, too. He and Hawkeye traded questioning looks. Then Mr. Collins cleared his throat and said, "By the way, I ran into Sergeant Treadwell today. He told me they caught the crooks who robbed the appliance store last Monday. They still haven't recovered the stuff that was stolen, though."

Mrs. Collins lifted her head and looked at her husband. "I'm sorry, Peter. What did you say?"

"What's wrong, Mom?" Hawkeye asked.

"You didn't even yell at me when I slipped Nosey some of my lamb chop. And I know you saw me do it!"

Mrs. Collins looked at Hawkeye and smiled. "I was thinking about something else," she admitted. "I've got a problem."

"What kind of problem?" asked Hawkeye.

"It's the Stevenson house," his mother replied. "As you know, the family moved out last month."

Linda Collins was a real estate broker. She worked for Town and Country Realty and sold houses in the Lakewood Hills area.

She shook her head. "Although it needs new locks on the doors and a few other repairs, the house is basically in good shape. But I can't find a single buyer for it. No one will even look at it!"

"Why not, Mom?" Hawkeye asked.

Mrs. Collins hesitated a moment, then said, "Well, there have been some strange noises."

"Noises!" Hawkeye exclaimed. "What kind of noises?"

"People who live in the neighborhood say they've heard eerie noises coming from the house at night," said his mother, "and now a rumor has gotten around that the house is haunted!"

"That's crazy!" Hawkeye said, laughing. "Everybody knows there're no such things as ghosts."

"It *is* crazy," Mrs. Collins agreed. "But this

kind of thing is really bad for business."

"Did you search the house?" Hawkeye wanted to know.

"From the basement to the attic," Mrs. Collins replied. "All I found was some furniture the Stevensons left behind. I certainly didn't find a ghost!"

Hawkeye gently tapped his fork against his plate. Then he asked, "Mom, what time do people start hearing these noises?"

"At exactly eight-thirty every evening. Why?"

"I just wondered," Hawkeye replied. "Is it OK if I start clearing the table?"

"Of course, dear," said his mother.

As Hawkeye carried a load of dirty dishes to the kitchen, he heard his mother say, "Peter, I simply don't know what to do!"

Hawkeye hurried to his room and looked at the digital alarm clock next to his bed. Then he turned out the lights, picked up his flashlight, and went to the window. With his hand, he wiped off a pattern of frost that had formed on the windowpane. Pointing the flashlight into the darkness outside, he flashed it, then paused. He counted to five and flashed it again.

"C'mon, Amy," he murmured. "Answer my signal."

A few seconds later, Amy's answering signal flashed back at him from across the street.

Still holding his flashlight, Hawkeye ran back downstairs.

"Hawkeye, we're leaving now," Mr. Collins said when Hawkeye bounded into the kitchen. Every Thursday night, the Collinses played bridge with their next-door neighbors.

"OK, Dad," Hawkeye said. "Have a great time. I won't be lonely. Amy's coming over."

"That's nice," his mother remarked. "Just don't forget to finish your math homework."

"I won't, Mom. Bye."

After his parents left, Hawkeye jerked open a kitchen drawer and grabbed another flashlight. Then he ran into the front hall. Just as he was getting a key to the Stevenson house from his mother's desk, Amy arrived. She was wearing purple corduroy pants, a wool turtleneck sweater, and her red parka.

"Wow, it's really cold out!" she exclaimed as she came in the door. "So what's up? I got your signal to come over and bring my bike."

Hawkeye handed her one of the flashlights. Amy looked at it.

"What's this for?"

"We're going ghost-hunting!" Hawkeye answered as he zipped up his dark green down jacket. "At the Stevenson house."

Amy stared at him. "We're *what? Where?"* she asked in disbelief. Then she laughed. "Oh, c'mon, Hawkeye. Everybody knows there're no such things as ghosts!"

Hawkeye nodded. "That's what I told my mom," he said.

"Your mom believes in ghosts?" Amy asked doubtfully.

Hawkeye wound a yellow-and-red-striped scarf around his neck. "Come on," he said. "I'll tell you all about it on the way."

The Stevenson house was about a mile and a half away. As they rode their ten-speeds through the cold December night, Hawkeye filled Amy in on the conversation at the dinner table.

"What a bummer," Amy said sympathetically. "I sure hope we can help your mom, Hawkeye!"

Ten minutes later, Hawkeye and Amy were riding up the steep, winding driveway that led to the Stevenson house. Their breaths left frosty trails behind them in the icy air. Every once in a while, the thick clouds surrounding the moon moved aside, and the two sleuths could see the house silhouetted against the wintry sky.

Amy shivered. "This place would look great in a horror movie," she commented as they parked their bikes next to the back door.

"Really," Hawkeye agreed. He shone his flashlight on his watch. "It's 8:28," he said. "The noises are supposed to start in two minutes."

As quietly as possible, Hawkeye unlocked the back door. "Boy, this lock is really rickety. You hardly need a key to get in," he muttered as they tiptoed into the kitchen. There they took off their gloves and unzipped their jackets.

"Maybe the noises are caused by the wind—or a creaky shutter or something," Amy suggested hopefully when they got to the living room.

"We'll soon find—"

Suddenly, a ghostly wailing sound filled the entire house. Then it stopped abruptly.

"Haw-Hawkeye," Amy whispered. "What was that?"

"P-Probably just the wind," replied Hawkeye in a shaky voice.

"Ooohh . . . . Ooohh . . . . Get ooouut . . . . Get ooouut . . . ."

"There it is again," gasped Amy. "Hawkeye, this place *is* haunted!"

Hawkeye was looking up the staircase. "I think it's coming from up there," he said. "I—I guess we'd better check it out."

Using their flashlights to light the way, Hawkeye and Amy crept slowly up the stairs. They were just at the top step when they heard it again: "Ooohh . . . . Get ooouut . . . . It's myyy hoouusse . . . . Get ooouut . . . ."

Amy spun around. "Hawkeye, I don't know if I can go through with this!" she whispered. "I haven't been this scared since that time we investigated the Moody mansion!"

"Me, either," Hawkeye said nervously. "It sounds as if it's coming from that room down the hall. Let's take a look." Then he stepped back, grinning. "After you, Amy."

"No way! *You* first," said Amy as she gave him a firm shove.

"Just send my body to my folks," Hawkeye joked weakly.

By the time he shone his flashlight into a tiny room at the end of the hall, the eerie voice had stopped again. Without thinking, Amy tried the light switch. When she flicked it on, light flooded the room.

"That's weird," Hawkeye remarked, scratching his head. "You'd think they would have turned off the electricity."

"I like this room much better with the light *on,*" Amy said. "I think I'm even starting to breathe normally again."

Amy and Hawkeye looked around the room. It had a slanted ceiling and one window, which looked out on the house next door. In the corner were a broken rocking chair and a battered-looking end table.

"I'm positive the noises came from this room," Hawkeye insisted.

He took off his jacket and dropped it on the floor. Then he took out his sketch pad and pencil.

"Amy, I'm convinced there's no ghost," Hawkeye said. "There's got to be a logical explanation for all this. I'm going to make a sketch of this room for us to look at later."

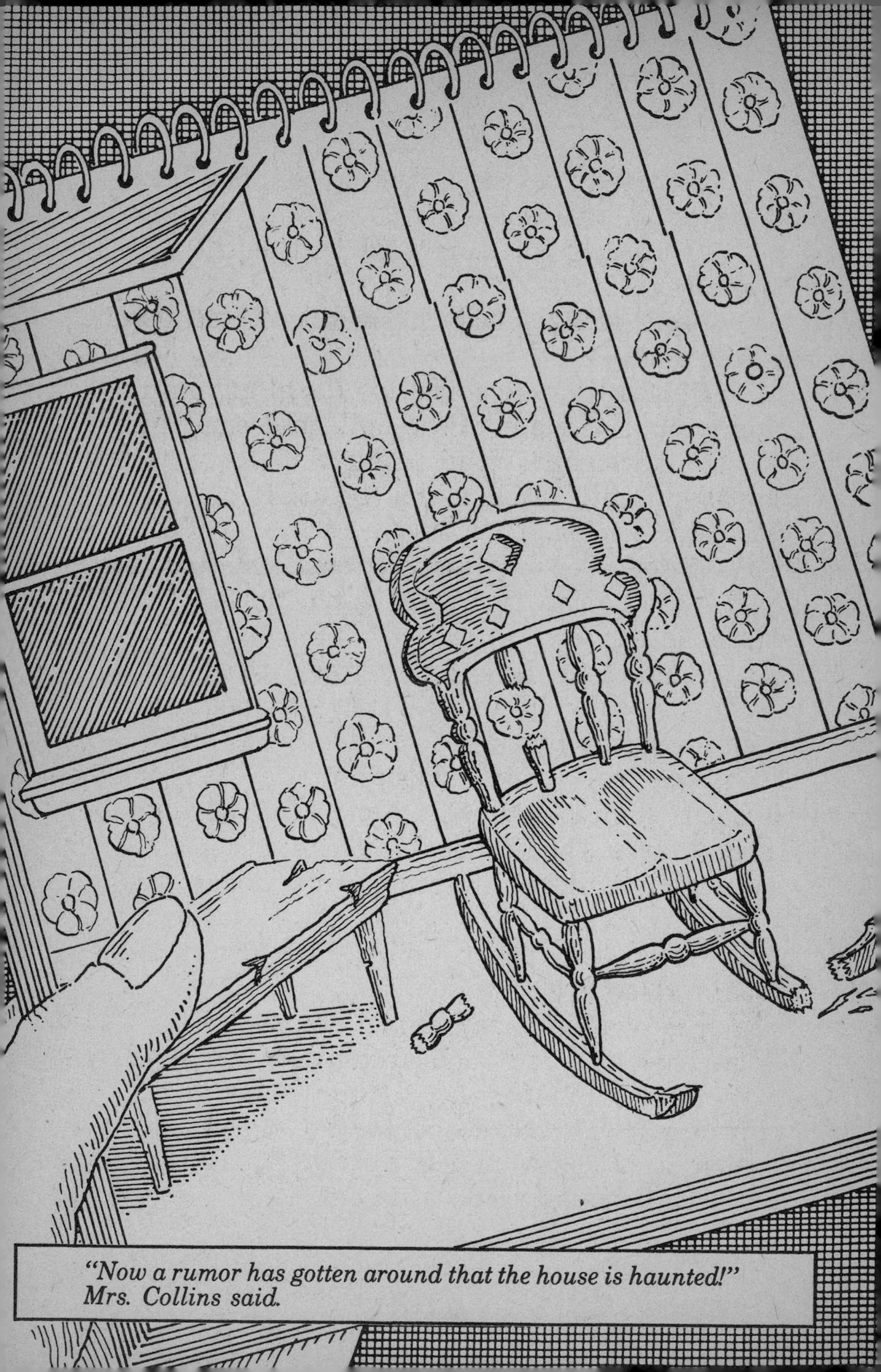

"Now a rumor has gotten around that the house is haunted!"
Mrs. Collins said.

"Good idea," Amy replied. "We ought to get out of here soon, or the neighbors will see the light on. Then they'll think there really are ghosts here!"

After Hawkeye finished drawing, he handed the sketch to Amy and put his jacket back on.

Amy looked at what Hawkeye had drawn. Suddenly, she gasped in amazement. "Hawkeye!" she exclaimed. "Look at this!"

She showed the sketch to Hawkeye, who stared at it. Then he started to grin.

"So that's where the 'ghost' is hiding!" he said.

WHAT WAS THE HIDING PLACE THAT HAWKEYE'S SKETCH REVEALED?

SOLUTION

See page 79

The Case of the Safari Slipup

Hawkeye and Amy were biking up the driveway of the von Buttermore mansion.

"Did you find out why Mrs. von Buttermore invited us to lunch?" Amy asked.

"Not really," Hawkeye answered, "but she was sure having a great time being mysterious about it. The invitation was delivered by Henry, her butler. It invited us to a small luncheon, with a side dish of good news!"

Amy laughed. "The good news is that a small luncheon at Mrs. von Buttermore's is usually five courses long!"

"If it were five courses of something *you'd* dished up," Hawkeye teased, "it would be good news if everyone didn't croak!"

"Croak!" Amy yelled, pretending to be angry. "What do you think I'd serve—frogs?"

Mrs. von Buttermore was the wealthiest person in town. She was also one of the nicest. And she had grown especially fond of Hawkeye and Amy.

"Amy! Hawkeye!" she bubbled when the two arrived at the house. "How good to see you! I've had the table set up outside. Follow me."

As Mrs. von Buttermore led her guests onto the patio, Amy whispered to Hawkeye, "I hope her news has something to do with the way she's dressed."

Their hostess was wrapped in brightly colored cotton clothing and wore a matching head scarf. Even for Mrs. von Buttermore's unusual taste, the outfit was a little stranger than they'd seen before.

"It does," Hawkeye said. "Look at the setting for our lunch!"

The tablecloth and the napkins were decorated with black-and-white zebra markings. The chair pillows were made of imitation leopard-skin material. Instead of an umbrella over the table, there was a thatched roof, and there were African-looking decorations all around the patio.

"Now," Mrs. von Buttermore said, "guess where I'm going!"

"If it's not Africa, then I'd better quit doing

detective work," Hawkeye said, laughing.

Mrs. von Buttermore laughed, too. "I suppose I did get a bit carried away, didn't I? But I'm so thrilled. I'm going on a safari!"

"You're going big-game hunting?" Hawkeye gasped.

"Oh, no! It's a safari to *watch* the animals, not to kill them. Two years ago, I got to see tigers in Asia, and kangaroos in Australia. This time I won't be able to see those animals, but I'll get to see all the wild animals that live in Africa."

"Are you going alone?" Amy asked.

"No, no. It's a group trip," Mrs. von Buttermore explained. "I'm on the board of directors of the Lakewood Hills Zoo, you know, and every year we have some kind of outing. This year is the zoo's thirtieth anniversary, so we all wanted to do something special.

"Well, when I suggested that the Zoo Society sponsor a safari, you'd have thought I'd tossed a bolt of lightning into the room. Everyone said it was the best idea ever brought up!"

"Won't a trip like that require a lot of planning?"

"Of course!" exclaimed Mrs. von Buttermore. "There are passports to get, equipment to rent, clothing to buy, and reservations to make. But, really, I think I have the *most* important job—choosing a safari guide!

"Now, sit down. You two must be as hungry

as a pair of young lions yourselves!"

As Mrs. von Buttermore arranged for the food to be served, Amy and Hawkeye looked at each other. They knew that Mrs. von Buttermore liked unusual things. Since the table setting was African, the food might be African, too!

"What if it's hippo meat?" Amy whispered, turning a little pale. "Or crocodile eggs?"

But they didn't have to worry for long. To their relief, the food wasn't strange. The soup, salad, vegetables, meat, and dessert were all familiar and delicious.

When the lunch was over, Mrs. von Buttermore took Hawkeye and Amy into her study. "I want to tell you about the safari guide I'm going to hire," she said as she leafed through a stack of papers. "Ah, here it is!" she said.

"This is the application of a Mr. Andrew Lumkin. He was born in England but has lived in Africa for most of his life. He's been a guide there for many years."

"Does he have any recommendations from people he's guided in the past?" Amy asked.

"Yes, several," Mrs. von Buttermore said. "Here's one of them: 'Mr. Lumkin is, in my opinion, the finest and most qualified guide available.'

"Here's another: 'Mr. Lumkin made our trip a joy. We never had a worry. He is an excellent guide, whom I would recommend for anyone's safari.' "

"This photo was taken in Africa, on the most recent safari he guided," explained Mrs. von Buttermore.

"Those are pretty good recommendations," Hawkeye said.

"Oh, I almost forgot!" Mrs. von Buttermore exclaimed. "I have pictures of him."

Reaching under her stack of papers, Mrs. von Buttermore pulled out several photos and handed them to Amy and Hawkeye. One picture was of Mr. Lumkin atop an elephant, and one showed him leaning against a palm tree. The third one showed him watching some tiger cubs.

"These photos were all taken in Africa, on the most recent safari he guided," explained Mrs. von Buttermore.

Both Amy and Hawkeye looked at the pictures closely. Amy tapped one of them against her palm as she studied it. Then she quickly handed it to Hawkeye.

"Hawkeye, what do you think?" she asked.

"I think the same thing you do," Hawkeye answered after he took a second look at the photo. "Uh, Mrs. von Buttermore, I hate to say this, but you'd better look for another guide."

WHAT DID HAWKEYE AND AMY SEE IN THE PHOTOGRAPH?

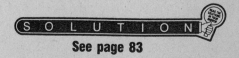

SOLUTION
See page 83

The Mystery of the Polite Prowler

Sergeant Treadwell was telling Hawkeye and Amy about one of his favorite crime-busting cases.

"So there I was," he chuckled, "dressed like an old bum. The thief walked right in front of me, probably looking for another purse-snatching victim.

"Well, you should have seen the look on his face when I asked for some spare change—and then clapped handcuffs on him when he stopped!

"Whoops, I've got a call," Sarge said, noticing his buzzing beeper. "The first time this thing went off, I jumped a mile. Now I don't mind it a bit." He looked a little embarrassed as he admitted, "In fact, it makes me feel like Dick Tracy!"

He walked to the corner and called police headquarters.

"Sarge missed his calling," Amy said. "The way he likes to disguise himself, he should have been an actor."

"Remember when he was investigating the muggings around the band shell? And the way he looked in that band uniform?" Hawkeye smiled at the memory. "I almost died laughing when he tried to play the tuba!"

"Yeah," Amy agreed, "and the conductor almost died of embarrassment!"

Just then, Sarge came back. "I'd love to chat some more, but I have to go out on a call. Seems there's been another break-in, this time at a Mr. Jameson's house. That makes four on the same block, in only three weeks!"

"Can we come along?" Hawkeye asked.

"I'm not sure . . . oh, all right," Sarge agreed.

Amy and Hawkeye climbed into his car.

"You knew Sarge would take us along, didn't you?" Amy said quietly to Hawkeye.

"Sarge may be a terror with criminals," Hawkeye murmured, "but he's a marshmallow with kids!"

Mr. Jameson was in his early twenties. By the looks of his house and the surrounding neighborhood, he was doing very well for himself.

As Sarge asked questions for his report, they

found out that Jameson was a computer consultant. He had a job setting up systems for businesses and private homes. Since computer systems are constantly being improved, Jameson had a good future. But right now, he was missing a roomful of computers.

"Can you describe the burglar?" Sarge asked.

"Oh, sure," said Jameson sarcastically. "He wore jeans, a long-sleeved shirt, and sneakers. He had on gloves, and he wore a ski mask. Some description, huh?"

Sarge had to agree it wasn't very promising.

"Could you recognize the burglar by his voice?" he asked.

"I wish I could," Jameson replied. "But he never said one word. I must say, though, he was the most polite burglar I've ever heard of!"

At the mention of the burglar's politeness, Sarge's ears pricked up. "Could you go through the whole burglary step-by-step, please?" Sarge asked.

"Well, it was late last night," Jameson began. "I'd been running some programs on my personal computers in the computer room I have, and I was tired. I went through the hallway into the living room.

"I noticed some glove prints around the windowsill in the hallway, but I didn't think much of it. I just wondered why the sill was so dirty when my housecleaner had been in only a couple of days earlier. Of course, that's how the burglar got in.

"As soon as I walked into the living room, the man came out of a dark corner. He showed his gun, and then he handed me a series of cards."

"What was on the cards?" Sarge inquired.

Jameson laughed. "Instructions! Everything was written out in order. The complete 'how-to'—for being robbed!

"The first card said he apologized for the inconvenience," Jameson said, "and hoped I wasn't worried. Each card after that said something different: 'Please put your hands behind your back so I can tie them' and 'Thank you for your cooperation.' "

"You were tied up?" Hawkeye asked.

"I sure was," Jameson answered. "Tied up and stuffed into my own closet. The burglar gave me a card that asked if the cord was hurting me. He apologized for making me uncomfortable, then he locked me in the hall closet!

"I had a terrible time getting my hands and feet untied. Then I had to get the closet door open. I almost yanked the knob off."

"Did you hear anything when you were inside the closet?" asked Amy.

"I heard him making off with my computers," Jameson moaned. "I heard him coming in and going out the back door, apparently loading the stuff into a truck or a car."

"Don't you have a burglar alarm system?" Hawkeye asked.

"Sure," Jameson said miserably. "It was switched off because I was home!"

"If it's any consolation, Mr. Jameson," Sarge said, "this isn't the first time we've heard a story like yours. It sounds like the polite prowler to me. Fourth time he's struck in this area!"

Unnoticed, Hawkeye slipped into the hallway with his sketch pad and pencil. He sketched the window where the thief had gotten in, and the closet in which Jameson had been locked. When he went back into the living room, Amy gave him a questioning look. Hawkeye shook his head slightly.

"You've been very helpful, Mr. Jameson, and we'll get on this case right away," said Sarge. "Don't worry. This guy will be behind bars soon!"

Almost as soon as they got outside, Sarge started planning a disguise as a yard worker.

"I'll get some old clothes from the flea market," he muttered, "and I've got some gardening tools at home. I can be looking for clues while I'm mowing lawns!"

"But doesn't the burglar usually strike at night?" Amy asked innocently.

Sarge sighed. "That's true."

Hawkeye had been looking over his sketch while Amy and Sarge were talking.

"Sarge," he said, "I think that for this crime,

"I noticed some glove prints around the windowsill in the hallway. That's how the burglar got in," said Mr. Jameson.

you've already seen the burglar. Jameson robbed himself! Look at my sketch, and you'll see what I mean."

When Hawkeye explained his reasoning, Sarge agreed, and headed back up the sidewalk toward Jameson's house.

WHY DID HAWKEYE SUSPECT JAMESON?

SOLUTION

See page 85

The Case of the Talkative Traveler

"Hi!" Amy called, catching up with Hawkeye on her ten-speed. "Where are you headed?"

"Billy's," Hawkeye answered. "Want to come along?"

"Sure. But I thought he was on vacation."

"Well, people *do* come back," Hawkeye laughed, "even from a place like Yellowstone National Park."

"Yellowstone!" Amy said a little enviously. "I'd love to see those fantastic rock formations some day, and Old Faithful, too."

"Oh, I don't know," Hawkeye said. "I sort of enjoy fantastic rock on my stereo, and my old faithful dog, Nosey."

"Is that supposed to mean *you're* not going anywhere special this summer?" Amy asked. "Well, me, either. But almost everybody else is out of town on vacation!"

Billy was in his front yard, working on his bike. "I really missed bike-riding," he told Hawkeye and Amy. "That's something I couldn't do in Yellowstone—the hills are just a little too steep."

Hawkeye was about to ask a question about Yellowstone when someone shouted from across the wide street. "Hi, mateys!" It was Charlie MacIntosh.

"Hi, Charlie," Amy said politely as he came over. "How was your summer camp?"

"No camps for me this year—I've been to Australia!"

"What?" Hawkeye exclaimed. "How'd you manage that?"

"I have an uncle who lives there. I'd never met him. But he wrote my folks that he wanted me to meet the 'dinkumest' side of the family—that's Australian slang for the best side.

"He was joking about that, but he wasn't joking about the visit. He sent round-trip plane tickets!"

"Everybody's been traveling. Billy went to Yellowstone," Hawkeye said.

"Oh, yeah, he told me," Charlie replied. "That's great. But you haven't seen a real desert until you've seen the Australian outback. We flew over it in my uncle's private plane."

"I went panning for gold," Billy said defensively.

"Gold?" Charlie interrupted. "I didn't look for gold, even though Australia had a gold rush just like the United States did. Gold's old stuff. We went hunting for uranium instead!"

Billy got an angry look on his face. "Bet you didn't meet any Indians," he said.

Charlie laughed. "No, but I did meet some aborigines, the native people of Australia. Do you know that—"

Billy jumped up. "No," he yelled, "and I don't want to!" He left his bike on the ground and stormed into his house.

Charlie shrugged. "Just jealous, I guess. Say, would you two like to come over to my house? I'm unpacking, and I've got some super stories I'd like to tell you."

"Not right now," Hawkeye said. "I want to see if Billy's OK."

When Charlie looked disappointed, Amy added, "Maybe we'll come over later."

"OK, sure," Charlie said, cheering up. "See you guys later, then. Don't take any wooden wombats!"

Hawkeye led Amy around the house to Billy's bedroom window. With a lot of knocking and gesturing, Hawkeye got Billy to come over to the window.

"Hey, what's the matter with you?" Hawkeye asked. "You and Charlie used to be friends."

"It's his twenty-four hour nonstop bragging. It's driving me crazy—especially because I don't think he even *went* to Australia! In fact, I'd bet my last nickel that he didn't!"

"You think he made the whole thing up?" asked a surprised Amy.

"Yes!" Billy answered. "The last two summers, Charlie's complained that his family doesn't take any big trips because his dad doesn't like to travel. It's hard to believe that suddenly this summer, they went halfway around the world.

"I wish you two would prove whether or not Charlie went to Australia. I could even take his bragging a lot better if I knew he had something real to brag about!"

Amy looked at Hawkeye. "Well, we said we'd visit him."

"See you later, Billy," said Hawkeye. "Don't take any—"

"I know, I know!" Billy interrupted him. "Wooden wombats!"

Charlie's bedroom walls were plastered with travel posters about Australia.

"I don't want to forget a thing," Charlie explained. "I had the greatest time of my life! We were on a ranch, and I 'fanged' it with the 'ringers' and 'jillaroos'! Oh, sorry. I picked up a lot of slang.

That means I ate with the cowboys and cowgirls."

"Did you see any kangaroos?" Amy asked.

"Did I ever! And I saw a real koala. And there was a weird animal called a platypus, and a bird called a kookaburra–here are some pictures." Charlie handed Amy and Hawkeye a handful of brochures.

"Don't you have snapshots?" Hawkeye asked.

"They're not developed yet," Charlie said quickly.

Charlie went on unpacking, singing an Australian song as he did so:

"Kookaburra sits in the old gum tree,
Merry merry king of the bush is he . . .

"Boy," he said as he unpacked his swimsuit, "did this get some good use! I learned to surf! A lot of the Australian kids are spending the whole summer surfing. They showed me tons of tricks. And Australia has some of the best surfing spots in the world."

Hawkeye didn't say anything. He had been quietly sketching the room while Charlie talked. Suddenly he looked up and glanced meaningfully at Amy. "Gee, Amy, it's almost time for lunch, isn't it?"

"Lunch? But I just had–" Amy caught Hawkeye's look and stopped in midsentence. "Oh, sure.

"Boy," Charlie said as he unpacked his swimsuit, "did this get some good use!"

"Well I guess we'll be going, Charlie. Thanks for having us over."

"Any time," Charlie said cheerfully.

Once outside, Hawkeye got on his ten-speed and raced toward Billy's house.

"Slow down, will you?" Amy panted.

"Sorry. But I've got big news for Billy."

"It's about Charlie's trip, isn't it?" Amy said. "He *did* make it all up! How did you figure it out?"

Hawkeye stopped. "Are you, Amy Adams, asking for *my* expert opinion?" he teased.

"I'm asking," Amy said "for a look at that sketch you did."

Amy did look at the sketch and then shook her head. "I don't see anything," she said finally.

"Elementary, my dear Amy," Hawkeye said in his best Sherlock Holmes imitation. "Charlie did a lot of research about Australia. And most of it is right on. But he made one mistake. An elementary mistake—elementary geography."

Amy's face lit up. "Of course," she said. "Let's go!"

HOW DID HAWKEYE AND AMY KNOW THAT CHARLIE'S VACATION WAS FAKED?

SOLUTION

See page 89

SOLUTIONS

SOLUTION

READ THE SOLUTIONS IN YOUR MIRROR

The Case of the Roman Coin

Mr. Bailey was not usually a careless man. But without his glasses, he failed to spot the flaw in the coin.

The date on the coin said 100 B.C., meaning one hundred years before Christ. But if it had been minted then, how would anyone have know about the existence of someone born a hundred years later?

Amy and Hawkeye broke the news to Mr. Bailey as gently as they could. Instead of being disappointed, he was grateful to the detectives.

"To think I would have ended up with a counterfeit coin without your help!" he exclaimed. "I am very grateful to you both. How can I repay you?"

"You already have," Amy replied. "This was a terrific visit, Mr. Bailey."

"You said it," Hawkeye added. "I didn't realize how interesting a hobby like yours could be!"

Mr. Bailey arranged to meet the coin dealer the next morning. When the dealer arrived, however, the only person he met was

continued

Sergeant Treadwell of the local police department.

The coin dealer got a jail sentence, and Amy got her hard-earned A for her research paper.

"There's something that still bothers me, though," Amy told Hawkeye the next week.

"What's that?"

"Well, you're the one who solved the counterfeit coin case for Mr. Bailey, and you're the only one who didn't really get anything for it."

"Wrong," Hawkeye said. "I've been talking with Mr. Bailey. He's promised to tell me how he got started collecting coins. This may have been a research paper for you—but I've found a whole new hobby!"

SOLUTION

READ THE SOLUTIONS IN YOUR MIRROR

The Case of the Rich Relative

Most of Hawkeye's sketches showed things that a nonhearing person would enjoy. There were lots of books around. There was also a television, but as Sarge pointed out, "That doesn't prove he's not deaf because he could have closed captioning, with what's being said also being printed on the screen."

"I know that," said Amy. "And I didn't see a phone, and I didn't see records or a stereo, either. But look in this corner."

"I'm looking—but what am I looking at?" Sarge asked.

"Something he could listen to music on, but which would be easy to hide at a moment's notice."

"I'll be darned!" Sarge exclaimed. "A Walkman! What would a deaf person do with one of those?"

Instead of going back to the man's house, Sarge decided to play cat and mouse. The next morning, "Mr. Mareno" came to the station house to sign claim papers. And that's when Sarge confronted the man with Amy's findings. At first, the man denied everything. But

continued

he soon broke down and confessed.

It seemed that the fake nephew had been a roommate of the real Daniel Mareno for several years. He knew, of course, about Mareno's deafness, and he had learned all about Mareno's family.

Mareno had moved to another state the year before. When the ad appeared, his former roommate decided to try to claim the fortune.

In a short time, the real Daniel Mareno was tracked down. He was so grateful to receive his inheritance that he wanted to share his good fortune. He contributed some of the money to a program that trained Lakewood Hills schoolteachers to include disabled children in regular classrooms.

READ THE SOLUTIONS IN YOUR MIRROR

SOLUTION

The Secret of the Mysterious Stranger

When Hawkeye looked at the photo, he started eliminating passengers who didn't fit the description of Pat McDonald. The man with the light suit couldn't be Pat, nor could the short, fat man or the dark-haired cowboy. In the picture of the passengers, only one person exactly matched the description. Pat McDonald was a woman!

"I took it for granted," Hawkeye said over dinner that evening, "that Pat was short for Patrick. I never even thought of it being a form of Patricia. And I imagined I remembered a Pat McDonald. I guess I just took that for granted, too, after hearing so many stories about a person with that name."

"I thought I would burst trying not to laugh every time you referred to 'Mister' McDonald," Mrs. Collins said.

"You weren't the only one," Mr. Collins added. "I actually had to leave the room once!"

"Well, I got a surprise, too," Pat said. "I had no idea that Christopher was such a grown person."

continued

"Would anyone like more pie?" asked Mr. Collins.

Hawkeye grinned. "Uh, Dad, that's one thing you always can take for granted—that you can give me a second helping of dessert!"

SOLUTION

READ THE SOLUTIONS IN YOUR MIRROR

The Secret of the Special Spies

"It's the part about your family's heroism," Hawkeye told Mark. "In 1790, when the letter was supposedly written, there weren't fifty states. There were only thirteen—from the thirteen original colonies!"

Mark opened his mouth as if to say something, then quickly snapped it shut.

"Gee, Mark, I'd think your parents would have noticed that mistake if this letter had been in your family a long time," Amy said.

Mark's face turned red, and he suddenly got very busy stuffing the framed letter into his backpack.

"Anybody—even you, Mark—could have written the letter on an old piece of paper and copied George Washington's signature," said Hawkeye.

"You two think you know everything!" Mark yelled angrily, and he stomped out of the cafeteria.

Hawkeye looked at Amy and shrugged. "I guess we'll be hearing a little less about Mark's family from now on."

SOLUTION

READ THE SOLUTIONS IN YOUR MIRROR

The Mystery of the Haunted House

Hawkeye's sketch showed a mismatched square of wallpaper.

On closer inspection, Hawkeye and Amy were able to make out an outline, and they found a small, flat button in the center of one of the wallpaper flowers.

"It's a secret door!" Amy exclaimed.

When they pressed the button, the door opened. As Hawkeye had suspected, there was no ghost inside. Instead, they discovered a tape recorder. When they rewound the tape and pressed the START button, the ghostly noises began again.

But that's not all they found. More tape recorders, as well as televisions and stereos, were stashed in the back of the room.

"I bet you anything this is the loot from the appliance store robbery," said Hawkeye. "The crooks must have set the tape to go off at the same time every night. They probably hoped people would think the house was haunted and not buy it. Well, they were right."

"Come on, Hawkeye," Amy said. "Let's go call Sarge. Then we can tell your mom the

continued

good news about the house!"

Hawkeye's mother was really angry that he had stayed out so late. But she was overjoyed when he and Amy told her what they had just discovered. She thanked them and gave them both a big hug. Then she promised not to ground Hawkeye—that time.

S O L U T I O N

READ THE SOLUTIONS IN YOUR MIRROR

The Case of the Safari Slipup

To Mrs. von Buttermore, the photos of Mr. Lumkin were proof of his honesty. And to Hawkeye and Amy, they were proof of his dishonesty.

"Mr. Lumkin may have led safaris before, but he's lying to you when he says that these pictures were all taken while he was on an African safari," Hawkeye told Mrs. von Buttermore. "Tigers are found in Asia, where you saw them, and in the jungles of South America, but there aren't any tigers in Africa. The snapshot of him and the cubs wasn't taken in Africa. It was taken either in another country—or in a zoo somewhere!"

"Good heavens!" Mrs. von Buttermore cried. "Thank you, Hawkeye. I'm so glad I didn't hire him! Well, there's one thing that Mr. Lumkin almost did that has to do with Africa."

"What's that?" Amy asked.

"He almost made a monkey out of me!"

SOLUTION

READ THE SOLUTIONS IN YOUR MIRROR

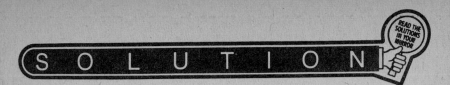

The Mystery of the Polite Prowler

"Did you forget something?" Mr. Jameson asked when he answered the door.

Sarge entered the hallway, armed with Hawkeye's sketch. "You say you pulled the closet door open from the inside?" he asked.

"That's right," Jameson answered a little nervously. "Is anything wrong?"

"Not much—except that you couldn't have pulled the door open from the inside," Sarge said. "You would have to have pushed it.

"And that's not all," Sarge went on. "Those glove prints on the windowsill are headed in the wrong direction. You said the burglar came in by the window and left by the back door. But the only way those prints could have been made is by someone inside!"

"You thought you could blame an already-existing criminal," said Hawkeye. "Then you'd collect insurance on the supposedly stolen computers and sell those same computers later on."

Faced with the facts, Jameson gave up and admitted his crime.

continued

Sarge did disguise himself as a gardener and sweated for several days planting shrubs, mowing lawns, and looking for the real burglar. Before the week was up, Sarge had caught the criminal.

"I'd like to say I always get my man," Sarge quipped to Hawkeye and Amy later, "but in this case, I can't."

"Why not?" Hawkeye asked.

"Because the polite prowler," Sarge explained, "was one of the sweetest old ladies I've ever arrested!"

SOLUTION

READ THE SOLUTIONS IN YOUR MIRROR

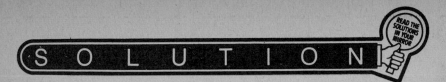

The Case of the Talkative Traveler

Charlie, tired of hearing his friends talk about their great vacations year after year, had taken a better vacation than any of them—in his imagination!

"It was one of his posters that tipped me off," Hawkeye explained to Billy. "Charlie couldn't have been surfing with Australian kids on summer vacation. It's wintertime in Australia when it's summer here!"

"And he couldn't come up with any snapshots," added Amy, "because there aren't any. And— Hey, Billy, what's the matter?"

"I never realized how hard it must have been for Charlie to hear about everyone else's vacations. We must have sounded to him just like . . ."

"Like he sounded to us?" Hawkeye said quietly.

"Yeah." Billy was silent for a moment. "How about letting Charlie think we believe him—just this once? Does that sound dumb?"

"It's not dumb," Amy answered. "It just proves you're the kind of guy who would never take any—"

continued

She stopped suddenly and grinned at the two boys.

"WOODEN WOMBATS," yelled Billy and Hawkeye together.

Dear Friend:

Would you like to become a member of the Can You Solve the Mystery?™ Reading Panel? It's easy to do. After you've read this book, find a piece of paper. Then answer the questions you see below on your piece of paper (be sure to number the answers). Please don't write in the book. Mail your answer sheet to:

Meadowbrook Books
Dept. CYSI-L
18318 Minnetonka Blvd.
Deephaven, MN 55391

Thanks a lot for your replies—they really help us!

1. How old are you?
2. What is your first and last name?
3. What is your address?
4. What grade are you in this year?
5. Are you a boy or a girl?
6. Where did you get this book? (Read all answers first. Then choose the one that you like best and write the letter on your paper.)

   6A. Gift
   6B. Bookstore
   6C. Other store
   6D. School library
   6E. Public library
   6F. Borrowed from a friend
   6G. Other (What?)

7. If you chose the book yourself, why did you choose it? (Be sure you read all the answers listed first. Then choose the one that you like best and write the letter on your paper.)

   7A. I like to read mysteries.
   7B. The cover looked interesting.
   7C. The title sounded good.
   7D. I like to solve mysteries.
   7E. A librarian suggested it.
   7F. A teacher suggested it.
   7G. A friend liked it.
   7H. The picture clues looked interesting.
   7I. Hawkeye and Amy looked interesting.
   7J. Other (What?)

8. How did you like the book? (Write your letter choice on your paper.)

8A. Liked a lot   8B. Liked   8C. Not sure
8D. Disliked   8E. Disliked a lot

9. How did you like the picture clues? (Write your letter choice on your paper.)

9A. Liked a lot   9B. Liked   9C. Not sure
9D. Disliked   9E. Disliked a lot

10. What story did you like best? Why?

11. What story did you like least? Why?

12. Would you like to read more stories about Hawkeye and Amy?

13. Would you like to read more stories about Hawkeye alone?

14. Would you like to read more stories about Amy alone?

15. Which would you prefer? (Be sure to read all the answers first. Then choose the one you like best and write the letter on your paper.)

15A. One long story with lots of picture clues.
15B. One long story with only one picture clue at the end.
15C. One long story with no picture clues at all.
15D. A CAN YOU SOLVE THE MYSTERY?™ video game.
15E. A CAN YOU SOLVE THE MYSTERY?™ comic strip.
15F. A CAN YOU SOLVE THE MYSTERY?™ comic book.

16. Who was your favorite person in the book? Why?

17. How hard were the mysteries to solve? (Write your letter choice on your paper.)

17A. Too easy   17B. A little easy   17C. Just right
17D. A little hard   17E. Too hard

18. How hard was the book to read and understand? (Write your letter choice on your paper.)

18A. Too easy 18B. A little easy 18C. Just right
18D. A little hard 18E. Too hard

19. Have you read any other CAN YOU SOLVE THE MYSTERY™ books? How many? What were the titles of the books?

20. What other books do you like to read? (You can write in books that aren't mysteries, too.)

21. Would you buy another volume of this mystery series?

22. Do you have any suggestions or comments about the book? What are they?

23. What is the volume number on this book? (Look on the front cover.)

24. Do you have a computer at home?

ORDER FORM

Name ____

Address ____

City _____________________ State ______________ Zip ______

Please charge my ☐ Visa ☐ Mastercharge Account

Acct.# ___________________________ Exp. Date __________

Signature ____

Check or money order payable to Meadowbrook Inc.

Qty	Title	Cost Per Book	Amt
	#1 The Secret of the Long-Lost Cousin	$2.75	
	#2 The Case of the Chocolate Snatcher	$2.75	
	#3 The Case of the Video Game Smugglers	$2.75	
	#4 The Case of the Mysterious Dognappers	$2.75	
	#5 The Case of the Clever Computer Crooks	$2.75	
	#6 The Case of the Famous Chocolate Chip Cookies	$2.75	
	#7 The Mystery of the Star Ship Movie	$2.75	
	#8 The Secret of the Software Spy	$2.75	
	#9 The Case of the Toilet Paper Decorator	$2.75	
	#10 The Secret of the Loon Lake Monster	$2.75	
	#11 The Mystery of the Haunted House	$2.75	
	#12 The Secret of the Video Game Scores	$2.75	
	TOTAL		

We do not ship C.O.D. Postage and handling is included in all prices. Your group or organization may qualify for group quantity discounts: please write for further information to Direct Mail Dept., Meadowbrook Inc., 18318 Minnetonka Blvd., Deephaven, MN 55391.

18318 Minnetonka Boulevard • Deephaven, MN 55391 • (612)473-5400